Excused myself to be away. Not adding the part I had to Act in
regard to my depar[illegible] ie
by a bloody Oath [illegible]
pull down my h[illegible]
to palliate this foolish menace, & though in [illegible]
humour, than exasperate on that Occasion, continued
in company till about four O'clock, then I retired Off
quietly, not imagining he should persist in his folly, went
to bed without dread or fear, as I gave no other plausible
offence except what some [illegible] suggested to them, but
the [illegible] ousness
of the [illegible] o'clock in
the m[illegible] said
the d[illegible] one plank
of th[illegible] to the
floor [illegible] broke down
my [illegible] s lay &
time [illegible] was principally
perpetrated, by Ens. Robert Johnstone of the 2d Battn.
& Oaks the leader; so fast was I asleep, knew nothing
of their violent proceedings, until Oaks surprized
me, out of a profound sleep, jumbling me roughly in
my bed, bawling loudly Doctor Doctor, damn your blood
rise, & give us a bowl of Toddy, otherwise you'll repent it,
I wakened as out of a Dream, to the said Oaks whose
question was if I had my dirk or [illegible] by my bed-side, I
answered, never in time of peace, upon this I called to
my servant,

PAGES FROM THE ORIGINAL MANUSCRIPT AS WRITTEN BY DANIEL MORISON, SURGEON'S MATE 2ND BATTALION, 60TH REGIMENT FORT MICHILIMACKINAC 1769—1772

"...swore by a bloody oath he would come with a Hatchet and pull down my house."

the DOCTOR'S *Secret Journal*

by DANIEL MORISON, *Surgeon's Mate*

Edited by George S. May

Illustrated by Dirk Gringhuis

Mackinac State Historic Parks
Mackinac Island, Michigan

ISBN-0911872-05-1

Private
BRITISH 60th FOOT ROYAL AMERICANS

Printed in the United States of America by
Harlo Printing Co., Detroit Michigan
Third Printing, 1969 15,000 copies
Fourth Printing, 1974 15,000 copies
Fifth Printing, 1984 10,000 copies
Sixth Printing, 1993 5,000 copies
Seventh Printing, 2001 3,000 soft cover - 1,500 hard bound

Introduction

On September 28, 1761, a year after France's vast North American empire had been surrendered to the British at Montreal, Canada, the flag of Great Britain was raised over Fort Michilimackinac, far to the west at what is now Mackinaw City, Michigan. A force under Major Robert Rogers, leader of the almost legendary Rogers' Rangers, had reached Detroit in 1760 and had taken control of that post, but the coming of winter had compelled the British to wait until the following year to take over the other French outposts in the upper Great Lakes.

Although Major Rogers later was to serve as commanding officer at Michilimackinac, the red-coated troops who marched into the little stockaded fort on the south shore of the straits connecting Lake Huron and Lake Michigan were commanded by Captain Henry Balfour. He found that the French garrison had departed for the west months before, leaving the fort in charge of Charles Langlade, a native of the area who had fought brilliantly on the French side during the French and Indian War. Balfour was greeted by several enterprising Englishmen who had gotten a head start in the race to gain control of the lucrative fur trade which for so long had been monopolized by French traders at Michilimackinac.

After accepting the fort's formal surrender and before leaving for the west, Balfour detailed a small force from the famous Royal American or 60th Regiment to remain as the garrison. Two years later, during the great Indian uprising of 1763, fierce Chippewa warriors massacred over half of the soldiers and temporarily drove the British out. But within a year they returned in greater numbers, and from then until 1781, when it was abandoned for a new, more easily defended post on Mackinac Island, Fort Michilimackinac was one of the key links in the chain of military and trading posts which Great Britain maintained on the western frontier of its American colonies.

Among those who came to the fort in the late 1760's was a Scotsman, Daniel Morison, surgeon's mate in the Royal Americans' Second Battalion. Of his life before and after his tour of duty at Fort Michilimackinac we know nothing. Under ordinary circumstances we would agree with one of Morison's commanding officers who told him bluntly, "You are not worth my Notice." But Morison is worth our attention because between 1769 and 1772 he kept a journal in which he set down in language that is often unintentionally hilarious and at other times brutally frank the best account that we have of life at this outpost of European civilization.

This important historical document, now published for the first time in its entirety, was purchased in 1914 by the great collector of materials relating to the history of Michigan and the Old Northwest, Clarence M. Burton, who bought it from a book seller in London, England, for $55. He brought the journal back to the state in which it was written where it now rests in the Burton Historical Collection of the Detroit Public Library.

Dr. Morison's journal provides us with a picture of the English population of the fort, a people beset by violence, lawlessness, tyrannical officers, petty bickering, and assorted other problems. A reading of the journal should dispel any romantic notions of what conditions were like at an eighteenth-century frontier fort.

The inhabitants of Michilimackinac consisted of several groups. There were the soldiers, numbering around a hundred men. A few of them, we learn from Morison, had brought out their wives. The commanding officer's house was the most impressive of the thirty-odd wooden buildings located within the stockade. The other officers lived in various cabins in the fort, as did the rank and file of the troops until 1769 when a large barracks was constructed in the center of the fort. Dr. Morison's complaints about the poor quality of the housing are supported by statements of others who commented on the ramshackle construction which necessitated constant repairs and made the danger of fire an ever-present fear.

As a military fort Michilimackinac was scarcely adequate even to withstand the attacks of Indians. The post was maintained, however, because it was a convenient center of the fur trade. The small garrison, with its six-pound and nine-pound cannon mounted on the bastions, was enough to impress the Indians who lived in the vicinity and those who gathered here each summer with the reality of British armed might. This symbol of military power protected the English fur traders who made up the second, and most important, segment of the fort's population.

By 1767 Michilimackinac had become for the British as it had been for the French the headquarters for the fur trade of a fourth of the continent. Canoes were sent out from here loaded with trade goods to be exchanged for furs at distant Indian villages located in the uncharted wilderness north and west of Lake Superior, westward across the Mississippi, and southward to the Illinois country. For two or three months in the summer hundreds of voyageurs *and traders came back from the west, bringing in the furs they had gathered during the previous year or two. Like the lumberjacks of a later era, these men were bent on enjoying to the fullest degree their brief contact with the comforts of civilization before they returned to the west to barter for more furs.*

A few traders who had acquired sufficient means to enable them to hire others to do the actual trading remained here the year round and occupied cabins in the fort. These Michilimackinac traders, men like Benjamin Frobisher, Isaac Todd, George McBeath, and others not mentioned by Morison, together with their agents or partners in Montreal who obtained the trade goods and sold the furs, dominated the fur trade for decades.

From Morison's narrative we see that the officers and the traders permanently in residence at the fort formed an elite group. It is obvious that the French habitants *and half-breeds who comprised a third part of the fort's population, not to mention the Indians of the area, were not admitted to this exclusive social club. That the strain of being cooped up in the small fort, cut off from all contact with the outside world for over half the year, proved too much for some of the members of this clique, especially the bachelors, is also obvious.*

Equally apparent is the fact that Dr. Morison, poor man, was unsuited to withstand the rigors of life at this post. He was apparently an educated man who could quote accurately from Virgil's Aeneid, *and a man of refinement and sensitivity. To some of the cruder members of the English set he must have seemed an easy target and a source of amusement when life became too dull and the bowls of toddy ran dry. Feeling himself much persecuted, as he certainly was, and outraged by the injustices of which he and others were the victims, Dr. Morison fumed, but, with a few exceptions, as when he refused to permit the whipping of a soldier to continue, he lacked the courage necessary to stand up to his oppressors. So, like Lieutenant Maryk in* The Caine Mutiny, *who kept a secret log on the activities of his sick captain, Dr. Morison recorded in his journal the evidence which he no doubt hoped would some day enable him to bring Ensign Robert Johnson, Captain George Turnbull, and his other tormentors to justice.*

Actually, Dr. Morison probably was not a doctor at all. He was a surgeon's mate, which means that he may once have been an apprentice to a surgeon and that he may have taken a course or two at a medical school but that it is unlikely he ever graduated since had he done so he would not have been simply a mate. The professional ability of the British army surgeon's mate was of a notoriously low order, and, if we may believe one of the Royal Americans' regimental surgeons, Daniel Morison was no exception in this respect. Surgeons were scarce, however, and a small frontier garrison, even when, as at Michilimackinac, it had been plagued by much sickness, had to be satisfied with the services of a mate. Unlike the surgeon, who was commissioned by the king, the surgeon's mate was only a warrant officer appointed by the colonel of the regiment. The mate, therefore, was inferior in rank even to the ensign, the lowest of the commissioned officers. This was undoubtedly the source of many of Morison's problems. He claimed the title of doctor and demanded equal status with the officers, who, for their part, treated him as they would a common soldier.

Comments added at the end of the manuscript in a different handwriting indicate that someone in England who possessed Morison's journal in the nineteenth century intended to publish it in a magazine. No evidence has been found that this was done. In preparing the journal for publication we have ignored the numerous changes that this earlier editor made in the document and have retained Morison's own phraseology at all times, including the misspelled words and grammatical construction so typical of his age. The narrative has been broken into five parts, and paragraphing and punctuation has been supplied at some places in the interest of easier reading. Material within brackets has been inserted by the present editor.

GEORGE S. MAY

Lansing, Michigan
March 6, 1960

"Doctor, damn your blood, get up & give us a bowl of Toddy!"

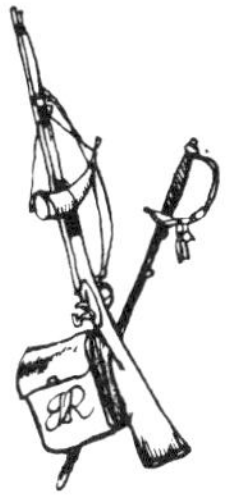

I

An Entertainment and a Violent Assault

Dr. Morison begins his journal innocently enough with an account of a party which he and others gave in the fall of 1769. Among the other hosts was Isaac Todd, who later helped found the great Canadian fur-trading firm, the North West Company, and whose long-time partner, James McGill, endowed McGill University in Montreal. The party began to get out of hand with the arrival of a couple of rowdy traders—John Chinn, who is best remembered as a partner in an unsuccessful copper-mining venture in Michigan's Upper Peninsula, and Forrest Oaks, who was a prominent fur trader at Michilimackinac and later at Montreal for a number of years after 1769.

Morison, who seems to have been something of a name-dropper, mentions as he goes along other men who are familiar to students of the fur trade and British military history. But all of them are dwarfed by Ensign Robert Johnson, who crashed Morison's party and soon turned the evening into a nightmare. Johnson (which is apparently how he spelled his name, although Morison insists on calling him Johnstone) is the villain of Morison's journal, a scoundrel and bully whom we come almost to admire for the infinite variety of ways in which he gave vent to his evil nature.

He had been deeply involved in the Robert Rogers affair which had rocked the little community at Michilimackinac two years before. Johnson was in Detroit in the fall of 1767 where he had gone for the treatment of an injury when a messenger from British military headquarters for North America arrived with orders to place Major Rogers, commandant at Michilimackinac, under arrest on suspicion of treason. Johnson brought these orders back to the Straits, and it was Lieutenant John Christie, an officer who also figures prominently in Morison's journal, who arrested Rogers. Johnson later asked to be given charge of the detail that took Rogers to Montreal for trial, boasting that he would foil any attempt that might be made to set Rogers free. However, when Rogers was acquitted, those who had hoped to see him convicted charged that the prosecution's case had been fatally weakened by Johnson's testimony which had enabled the defense to show that Rogers had been mistreated while he was a prisoner. Such mistreatment would be in keeping with the picture of Johnson's character which emerges from a reading of Dr. Morison's journal.

Narrative of an Action of Burglary and felony perpetrated on the Dwelling House & person of Daniel Morison, Surgeon's mate of the 2d. Battn. 60th Regt. at Michilamackinac the Seventh day of November (about 5 Oclock in the morning) in the Year one thousand seven hundred & sixty nine, Vizt:

That the evening before being the sixth of November, Isaac Todd, merchant, William Maxwell, commissary of provisions & I proposed to give an Entertainment at Sergt. [Thomas] MacMurrays to which we Severally invited such people as we thought (in such a remote corner) qualified to make the evening pass agreeably. Accordingly we met, and everything was carryed on with the greatest Decency & innocent Mirth till John Chinn & Forrest Oaks, traders, joined us.

After drinking a glass round, John Chinn (who appeared to be the worse of liquor) before & at supper began to be troublesome, opened upon me with Volleys of ragged raillery (without the least provocation on my side) and that blended with Opprobrious Expressions, namely, that I was an officer in the Rebellion &c. in the Year 1745 [the abortive Scottish attempt to place Bonnie Prince Charlie on the British throne], which tho' I knew was an arrant untruth, did not think it prudent to make the proper answer his wrongious Assertions deserved, [but] waved it off in the smoothest manner, lest the Company should be disturbed. Notwithstanding, our merriment was in a great measure unhinged, as the said John Chinn's only pleasure consisted chiefly in being officious, by hobb or nobbing with everyone [who] would chuse to drink with him, & indeed importunely pouring perpetually in upon those who did not chuse to drink more than would do them good.

About the hour of eleven o'clock, Ens. Robert Johnstone (who for ought I know invited himself) came in, accompanied by Ens. John Strickland & Mr. [George] Main. We continued thus till about one O'clock in the morning, when Numbers of our Company thought proper to retire. I proposed retiring also, but Isaac Todd insisted upon my spending one hour or two more with them. Rather than disoblige I consented.

About half one hour after, Ens. Johnstone asked the Company how their punch pleased them. They answered, well enough. Then he, the said Ens. Johnstone, blabbed out publickly, Vauntingly & wantonly, he had mingled four ounces of Jallap [a purgative] with the water that was a boiling for proportioning the Punch & Sangary [wine spiced and diluted with water]. This giddy Declaration, instead of meeting with approbation, occasioned the interjection of one universal sneer. I said nothing tho' I perfectly knew such irregular proceedings could not be intended for good. Therefore I silently winked over it, as others did; at the same time took particular notice that Ens. Johnstone drank nothing but wine all the night over.

John Chinn and Forrest Oaks, who left the Company about one o'clock, seemingly fuddled, returned to the charge one hour & one half thereafter. The abovesaid John Chinn appeared to be as unruly as ever. In short, conversation became very insipid. Drinking was the principal amusement, varnished over with various inconsistencys. At length time dragged on very heavily. Consequently [I] excused myself to be away, pleading the part I had to act in regard to my department. Upon which John Chinn swore by a bloody Oath he would come with a Hatchet and pull down my house, if I did not stay a little longer. To palliate this foolish menace, I thought it prudent to humour, [rather] than exasperate [him] on that Occasion.

[I] continued in [his] company till about four o'clock, then sheered off quietly not imagineing he would persist in his folly. [I] went to bed without dread or fear, as I gave no other plausible offense except what my absence suggested to them. But the Sequel will evidently discover the Maliciousness of their perverse intentions, for about five o'clock in the morning the seventh of November abovesaid, the door of my house was forcibly broke open, one plank of the Doorleaf, bars, bolt &c. pulled down to the floor. Upon entering my Room they also broke down my stove which was strongly made of bricks, clay & lime. This unwarrantable deed was principally perpetrated by Ens. Robert Johnstone of the 2d Battn. & Oaks the trader.

So fast was I asleep [that I] knew nothing of these violent proceedings untill Oaks Surprized me out of a profound sleep, tumbling in roughly in my bed [and] bawling loudly, "Doctor, Doctor, damn your blood, get up & give us a bowl of Toddy, other wise You'll repent it."

I wakened as out of a dream. He, the said Oaks' next question was if I had my durk by my bed-side. I answered, "Never in time of peace." Upon this I called to my servant John Forbes to light a candle, which was no sooner done, & set upon the table at my bed side after my servant retired to the kitchen, then the said Ens. Johnstone kicked down &

overturned the table, candle, candlestick, &c., topsy turvy in great wrath.

"Is this You, Ens. Johnstone," says I, "who behaves so rudely."

"You ly," he says, "I am a gentleman."

I made answer that his rude behavior betrayed the contrary in the eyes of good men.

Then he swore bloodily in the height of Rage, he would shew me that he was a gentleman & immediately fell upon, attacked & pelted me violently in my naked bed, he & his abbettor Oaks. The room being dark all my attempts of defence were rendered ineffectual by Oaks's exerting his outmost strength to entangle me in my sheets & bed-Cloathes out of which I struggled to extricate myself like a fish entangled in a net. They pelted me pell-mell with incessant blows repeatedly, on the face, left breast, &c., to the Effusion of my blood. Before I could recover myself out of the jeopardy into which I was involved, my shirt, sheets & pillowcase [were] all bespattered with gore & blood in my naked bed untill Sergt. McMurray & Arthur Ross, soldier, with the assistance of my servant, John Forbes, turned them out of the Room. Otherwise it is [hard] to know where the consequences would end. William Maxwell, the Commissary, & Christian Burgy, trader, came in who saw my face bruised all over, besmeared [with] Blood.

In the meantime Forrest Oaks had the impudence to come back again, & upon a rehearsal of my bad useage, very unmannerly gave me the ly twice or thrice, in my own house. To this Sergt. MacMurray, Mr. Maxwell & the abovesaid Christian Burgy was present, who can testify in this, as well as other Circumstances. I imagined he intended this insult as a provocation to stirr me up to do something rash, of which he might make a handle to invalidate my pretensions to Justice on account of his being accessory to the violent attack upon my person as abovesaid.

Whether there were more accomplices [who] acted in conjunction with Ens. Johnstone & Forrest Oaks at the breakeing of my house &c., I cannot positively determine (the room being dark) except what may be inferred from a chain of Circumstances. For John Chinn (whose mind it seems was so replete with the dregs of his former menaces abovesaid, as if he intended to make his menace good) he, the said John Chinn, was met by Isaac Todd on his way to my house, with a great Hatchet in his hand. Mr. Todd asked where he was going. The said John Chinn answered, to break down the Doctor's house. Upon which Mr. Todd, partly by persuasion, & partly by dint of strength, brought him home to his lodgeing.

Whether it was before this, or after, I cannot say, my servant John Forbes catched the said John Chinn at the porch before my broken door, with a large Hatchet, while the assailants abovesaid, to wit, Ens. Johnstone & Oaks, were perpetrating their malicious designs against me. He, the said John Forbes, asked the said John Chinn what was he going to do with that Hatchet. John Chinn replyed, to break down the Doctor's house. After a little altercation my servant persuaded him to deliver up the Hatchet.

No sooner the assailants abovesaid was expelled the house, as above mentioned, then the said John Chinn entered my house abruptly, as straight as a rush, & with an air of authority, impudently (tho' he saw my face &c. all over with blood besmeared) minding his belly more than my hard treatment asked if I should give him a bowl of Toddy, in presence of Mr. Maxwell & Mr. Burgy.

When these irregular proceedings perspired [*sic!*] the most considerable gentlemen in the Garrison came to see me, to wit, Capt. [Beamsley] Glazier [commandant, 1768-70], Lieut. Nordberg, Lieut. [John] Christie, Ens. Strickland, Mr. Todd, Mr. Main, Mr. [Charles?] Morison, Mr. Maxwell & Christian Burgy, who can all & one of them attest they plainly saw that the door of my house &c. were forcibly broke open as abovesaid, & that my face &c. was all over besmeared with blood & gore, & my shirt, sheets, pillowcase, were plentifully bespattered with blood also.

John Chinn, upon Recollecting what he had done, [realized he had] forgot his Hatchet, which he was very impatient to have in his possession once more, as it was then in custody of my servant John Forbes for about half one hour. The said John Chinn employed Christian Burgy, abovesaid, to bring it back to him. I did not chuse to give it, but upon the said Christian Burgy's earnest Expostulations I complyed, & ordered my servant to deliver it. At the same time [I] told Christian Burgy it was to the same purpose, as he & my servant could testify with Isaac Todd, [to] the maliciousness of his [Chinn's] unwarrantable intentions as abovesaid.

Soon after Ens. Johnstone & his abbettor Forrest Oaks had been expelled my house, he, the said Ens. Johnstone, went to Ens. Strickland's. The abovesaid Isaac Todd happened to be there, who upon Johnston's appearing, observed blood upon his hands &c. [Isaac Todd] asked him, where he had been. The said Ensign Johnstone replyed Vauntingly, he was giveing some knocks to the Doctor.

About half one hour after seven the evening before, Ens. Johnstone with some other accomplices were discovered scaling up a ladder opposite to which there was a half door, up the loft, at the lower end of my house. My servant John Forbes & another soldier observing a noise, as if the half door was thrown down upon the loft, [started out] but before my servant & the other soldier could get out to make a real discovery, the attempters were scattered about different ways. What their intentions were in regard to this little Enterprise depends upon them to explain but the judicious may readily conclude it a prelude to their malicious perpetrations before daylight next morning.

Before, at, or about six weeks preceeding the 7th November abovesaid, there was a strong report prevailed in [the] Garrison (which I am now persuaded was not without foundation) that the said Ens. Johnstone, being in company with some gentlemen in the fort, had breathed out menaceing and malevolent expressions against me, threatening he would use me ill.

Ens. Johnstone's reasons for this extravagant Declaration I am yet a stranger to, as it is conscious to myself I never did in word or deed give him any just grounds of provocation. Notwithstanding this surmise, I took no further notice of [it] than studying to evade his Company, excepting behaveing with common civility on general terms, as I knew his Character among the public to be of a turbulent & troublesome, meddling [and] loquacious Disposition.

Upon the whole, I believe, it will not be attended with much Difficulty to investigate sufficient evidences, who will attest to the Veracity of the above, when they are legally called upon to declare their Sentiments, Solemnly without the least partiality or mental reservation in presence of any competent Tribunal, by which it will evidently appear (to the Judicious) with other concurring Circumstances that the forcibly breaking up of my house &c., together with the violent assault upon my person as above specifyed, may be justly attributed to premeditated & malicious intentions. Authentick witnesses to prove the last assertion are Isaac Todd, Benjiman Roberts, late Lieut. in the 46th Regt., Benjiman Frobbisher, merchant, & William Maxwell, Commissary of Provisions in this Fort.

N. B.: When Sergt. McMurray & Arthur Ross came into my house they found Ens. Johnstone holding my servant by the hair of his head & pelting at him with several knocks altennarly [alternately?] for attempting to force him out of the house, which he got accomplished with the assistance of Sergt. MacMurray & Arthur Ross.

N. B.: That in the month of March 1766, he [Johnson] threatened he would break my head. No sooner [did] I put myself in a position of Defence, but he desisted from his insolent menaces. Proof: Lieut. Allan Grant of the 2d. Battn., Lieut. Varingon & Adjutant Biron [John Burrent], both of the 1st. Battn. 60th Regt.

II

Concerning the Most Irregular Proceedings

Daniel Morison was so incensed by the events related in the preceding narrative that he wrote out two versions, which, however, with the exception of an occasional difference in wording are the same. Following these events, from time to time he recorded some of the "irregular proceedings" which transpired at the fort, largely as a result of the actions of the irrepressible Ensign Johnson.

Morison's journal illustrates vividly how completely the military authorities dominated the lives of the fort's inhabitants. Not only were the soldiers at the mercy of their officers, but civilians, such as Morison's nephew, William Morison, were helpless in the face of military indifference to their problems since there was no civil authority at Michilimackinac or anywhere else in what is now Michigan to which they might appeal during this period. Traders constantly complained at the high-handed actions of the fort's commanders who, these traders charged, used their position to gain great material benefits for themselves and imposed ruinous regulations on those traders who would not give them a cut of their profits. The royal government sought to correct these abuses, but throughout the period of British rule Michilimackinac is said to have had a reputation as a center of corruption and misrule.

"Ensign Johnstone (who was there with his wife) saluted him with innumberable knocks & kicks."

Remarks December 1769.

[1stly.] That a few days after this unwarrantable Outrage perpetrated against my dwelling House & person, John Chinn & Forrest Oaks were so conscious of their Enormous guilt [and] struck with such a Remorse, that they declared that they would upon their knees publickly on the Parade beg to be pardoned if that would satisfy for the Errors they were conscious of haveing committed. This they expressed in the Audience of William Maxwell, Commissary, Sergt. McMurray, George McBeath, [and] Henry Williams, traders.

2dly. That a certain gentleman heard it surmised among them that if the above Submission would not take place, they might have another Resolve which was to tamper with my Servant & advance him one hundred pounds by way of bribe, as they looked on him as the most Material witness in my intended process against them.

3rdly. Such is the depraved disposition of this profligate Garrison at this Juncture (as well as now degenerateing into the most irregular proceedings dayly) they had recourse to calumnious aspersions contriveing to patch up false invective & ignominous Reports (as under the Necessity of keeping my room, on account of the Severe [bruises] I had sustained from such a rough handleing, that I wore Boots with Creepers in my Room & [was] found lying down in my bed with them); with this additional & abominable connivance that I kept so long close in my Room to embrace one opportunity to drive away Sorrow & get drunk privately. Such are the Diabolical dispositions of many in this remote garrison who make a perpetual habit of murdering time in excesses of Debauchery & most Licentious practices. These false aspersions I had communicated to me by George Main and Charles Morison, trader, the 10th December, 1769.

4thly. Upon the 11th do. Ens. Johnstone assumed to encroach upon my Province by visiting Sergt. McPherson of the Colonel's Company, who says he never sent for him Directly or indirectly. He immediately insisted upon seeing his wound, tho' he was but newly dressed one hour before,

[and] took off the dressings, &c. After inspection he told my patient for his comfort, it looked very bad, & that he knew nothing better for him than to bathe it with brandy. [He] set off directly, & left the tumefyed wound exposed to the Open air, till my servant was obliged to go & dress him a second time. This among the rest is one specimen of the Ens. Johnstone's activity to interfere in matters which did not concern him. That at the same time he told Sergt. McPherson if he belonged to the Company, he [would give] commands. He would immediately confine Dr. Morison in the common guard house.

N. B.: That in a few days after this Violent Assault, John Chinn and Forrest Oaks were observed conjointly & severally, loading their guns & pistoles, which I dare say were intended for bad purposes which they would in all appearance have prosecuted had not their proceedings been disapproved of by a certain gentleman in the Garrison.

One night the ensueing spring, when they carroused heartily at their Bowl, John Chinn proposed to pay another Visit to the Doctor, which being disapproved of by one of the principals in the Assault, was dropped.

The 25th. December 1769. Ens. Johnstone with his irregular associates, contrived among them, about day set in the evening, to send a frenchman, who served Isaac Todd merchant, upon a false Message to me two different times in great haste, acquainting me that his master was very sick, & that he earnestly, in the most pressing manner, demanded my immediate assistance. Upon which I Repaired directly to wait upon Mr. Todd, & upon due enquiry, found the Message to be a mere bubble, very like the triffling projectors, Isaac Todd declareing himself well, & took it highly amiss that they should take such libertys with his name, or give me such Unnecessary trouble.

Some time in Summer 1770, Ens. Johnstone Knocked down a soldier of the general's Company, called Walker by name, in presence of the Commanding officer, Capt. [George] Turnbull. The poor soldier applyed to me, & told me he was afraid his cheek bone was broke, which did not happen to be the case, tho' it was prodigiously swelled. Which cost me five or six days attendance and applications, before he recovered so as to be fit for Duty.

Sunday evening at 11 O'clock, 2d. December 1770, a frenchman knocked at the door of my house very hard, when I was abed. Imagining it Might be from some sick soldier, [I] called to my servant to open the Door, & there appeared a frenchman with a card in his hand, charged with Mr. Chinn's Compliments to Doctor Morison, begging the favour of his Company to take a dance with them at Christian Burge's house. This I rejected with outmost derision & Contempt, as I never did prostitute my Judgement so low as to join Company of any Denomination to break the Lord's day in such a publick [and] infamous manner; & indeed I looked upon the Company so mean that I should be very scrupulous to join them even on a Weekly day. I doubt not but Ens. Johnstone might be at the head of such a Heathenish proposition as there is no irregularitys committed here, wherein he is not either a prompter or a ready Countenancer if not a perpetrator.

Sunday the 9th December 1770. Betwixt the hours of 11 & 12 o'Clock forenoon, when the Garrison was at Church, Sergt. [Thomas] Carlile of the general's company had the guard that day, & being thirsty stepped over to his own house (which was adjacent & directly opposite to his guard) for a drink of spruce beer. He no sooner opened the Door of his room than Ens. Johnstone (who was there with his wife) saluted him with innumberable knocks & kicks till (almost in his own words to me) he had knocked his head into blubber, then kicked him in the private parts (from which Violence his private parts, particularly one of his testicles, are greatly Swelled, of a hue black as his Hat). [Johnson gave him] many bumps upon his head, [and] his jaw bones, as he himself says, [are] so painful that he can scarce open his mouth, but with great difficulty.

The poor Sergt. immediately returned to his guard & the next day applyed to the commanding officer Capt. Turnbull of this Fort for his Protection in regard to his most grievious situation, from the Attrocious and barbarous usage he had sustained by the violent proceedings of Ens. Johnstone whom he was determined to prosecute to the outmost for the Violence done to his person, in his own house.

N. B.: Ens. Johnstone confined two or three soldiers in the black-hole for being absent from Divine service, where they were in durance while he himself was pounding & kicking the poor Sergt. in this barbarous manner.

Late in the evening Sunday above said, Ens. Johnstone was swaggering away upon the Parade with a naked sword, or Dagger, in his hand, & when it seems he could not meet a Humane [*sic*] Subject to Use ill, he wrecked his Vengeance on a dog (belonging to one of the Soldiers of the Garrison) by cutting him to the back-bone. The poor brute made such a hideous noise, his wound being beyond Remedy, [that] his master was obliged out of Pity to put him out of pain by shooting him thro' the head.

Wednesday 12th December 1770. A little before Roll-Call Ens. Johnstone struck my servant, John Forbes, by giveing him several blows, which hurt him prodigiously, for attempting to ridd some Dogs that were a fighting & make[ing] a terrible Noise at the Door of my house. He struck Sergt. McMurray, acting Sergt. Major in the fort, with a severe blow, at the same time knocked down flat [on] the ground Henry Adams of the Collonel's Company, so that the dogs of this garrison are so Usefull, Sergents & Soldiers must be knocked down for attempting to hinder them from fighting & makeing a noise.

Ens. Johnstone kicked Sergt. McPherson of the Collonel's Company in presence of the Commanding officer, a little before he went down to Detroit last fall. Wednesday 26th December 1770, upon the evening of that day Ens. Johnstone knocked down Sergt. May upon the Parade, by giveing him two severe blows on the neck & Jawbones, after which he confined him, brought him to a tryal, & sentenced [him] to be reduced to the ranks.

On Saturday 29th, Do., Ens. Johnstone wrangled with my nephew, William Morison, erroneously & threatened to confine him in the common guard-house.

Sunday evening 30th Do., Mrs. [George] McBeath invited me to walk into her house. I was no sooner seated than she entered a grieveous Complaint to me against Ens. Johnstone, affirming that he used uncommon libertys with her Character, upon which she wrote him the evening before a very spirited Letter of which she shewed me a Copy. She actually pronounced him a very bad man. As a strong instance of which, among many she could adduce, she declared he had frequently tampered with her by many stratagems to destroy her peace with her husband, which she looked upon as such a vile insinuation she was determined never to admit of his Company for the future.

Tuesday evening the 1st. Jan'y 1771. John Savage, Taylor & Soldier in the general's Company, twixt 11 & 12, had the Door of his house forced open [and was] committed to the guard-house for not suffering his wife to comply with obscene proposit[ions made] to her. At this Exploit Ens. Johnstone was one of the chief witnesses. The prisoner was set at liberty next morning without any crime given against him.

Monday the 7th Jan'y 1771. Ens. Johnstone decoyed away Sergt. Carlile's wife, which he has been contriveing to accomplish many months before this finishing stroake, & tho' her husband was like to break his Heart, and crying out his Eyes on the occasion, Yet no Remonstrances would be payed the least attention to. Ens. Johnstone quitted his Room in the officer's barracks that evening which he exchanged with Mr. Main for his. [He] sleeped with her that night in his new room where he lives with her still, without dread or shame, while the poor Husband is left in such a disconsolate situation that is not easy to describe. He next morning (poor man) applyed to the Commanding Officer, who gave him no satisfactory redress, as he did not chuse to interfere either pro or con. Yet the next day after her Elopement from her husband she had the honnour of dining with the commanding officer and his mess, who drank tea with her that evening at her new lodgeings.

Sergt. Carlile had the mortification to see his wife dayly conducted by one of the mess to dine with the commanding officer, Capt. Turnbul, & the good Company with him, at which the poor Sergt. was like to go distracted but could not help himself.

Ens. Johnstone in the month [of December?] 1770, haveing crossed on a party of pleasure in company with Capt. Turnbull & William Maxwell, Commissary, flogged Knight, Soldier in the general's Company, with his own hand, without any regular tryal for his crime. Proof: William Maxwell, Commissary, Rogers & McLean, soldiers.

As Ens. Johnstone thought proper to turn trader by selling of common rum to the soldiers & all others by whom he might gain a penny in this clandestine Manner, in the month of October 1767, he was observed to have filled up several Barrels of common rum with boiling water to make up the Leakage. Afterwards [he] sold this at 18. sh. York currency pr. gallon to Sergeants & Soldiers &c. in the Garrison. Proof: Sergeants McMurray & Carlile with his own servant Arthur Ross, who assisted him by his own self in the deceitfull operation.

Upon friday the 8th febry. 1771, Ens. Johnstone in presence of the Commanding officer, Capt. Turnbull, Ens. Strickland, George Main, William Maxwell, Commissary, [and] George McBeath, trader, attacked William Morison, my nephew, in a most rude and Violent manner, without any evident cause, in the billiard Room in the presence of six witnesses. The Young man (who is sometimes liable to a fainting Disposition) in the Scuffle he fell down & cryed Murder! William Maxwell, Commissary of provisions, interposed, by which he received some knocks from Ens. Johnstone without returning one blow, after which Johnstone passed by [the] Commissary in a furious manner, & the young man was flat down in a swoon. Ens. Johnstone raised up his left arm & gave him repeated thumps opposite to the heart, by which it would appear he intended to murder the young man.

He is now under care & it is a chance if ever he can get the better of it. The commanding officer with all those of their Club was present to all this. Some of them I am told stood firm with their backs to the room door, I suppose to hinder any from comeing in to the assistance of the ill-used Young man. At length the noise brought in Mr. Harise, who can attest to everything he saw. Mr. Harise with one or two more carryed him for dead to his room, where after untying his stock he gradually recovered from his trance.

In the evening I went with my Nephew to wait on Capt. Turnbull to enter a Complaint of his hard usage. After all the remonstrances he could suggest, the Commanding Officer would give him no Redress, tho' he himself was personally present to the crime committed by Johnstone. Upon which I myself made application to Capt. Turnbull in the humblest manner to put Ens. Johnstone under arrest & that there was no possibility of maintaining peace in the Garrison while Johnstone was at liberty, nor could I think myself safe in the Execution of my Office if my Remonstrances to him on that score did not take place, which Capt. Turnbull Absolutely refused to do by saying, with some warmth, he would not put Johnstone under arrest, tho' there [were] as many crimes against him as words on his Commission.

The 23d. feby. 1771. Ens. Johnstone quarrelled with William Maxwell, Commissary, & revilled [him] (if not gave him a few blows) with exasperating expressions, both in company of the commanding officer, who, when words became too high, ordered Ens. Johnstone to his room, wherein he did not continue above twenty four hours, for reasons best known to the Commanding Officer & himself.

". . . a woman who I have the greatest regard for distracted me by her imprudent behaviour."

III

A Regimental Court-Martial

The little domestic tragedy involving Sergeant Thomas Carlile, his wife, and Ensign Robert Johnson, the first two acts of which transpired in the last chapter, now comes to an end with the utter defeat and humiliation of the poor sergeant.

Brought to trial on a charge of being disrespectful to an officer, Carlile sought to get his case tried not by a regimental court-martial, but by a general court-martial which would have a larger number of judges, including officers from other units, who would be more likely to judge his case without prejudice. With Ensign Johnson sitting as a member of the court it is not surprising that Carlile's request was denied nor that he was found guilty and reduced to the rank of private.

Carlile shortly was restored to his sergeant's rating but only after agreeing to take back his faithless wife and writing a letter at Johnson's order in which he abjectly begged forgiveness for daring to suggest that the ensign ought not to sit as a member of the court.

The record of Carlile's court-martial was stricken from the regimental orderly book, but Morison copied the proceedings as follows:

Michilamackinac, February 16th, 1771.
Proceedings of a Regimental Court Martial, 2d. Battn. 60th Regt. by order of Capt. Turnbull, Commandant.

President—Lieut. Christie

Prisoner, Sergt. Carlile

Ens. Johnstone, member

Confined by order of Ens. Strickland for being insolent & behaveing with Disrespect to him. Ens. Strickland informs the Court that he went a Carrioling [riding in a cariole, a kind of sleigh] with a Woman under his Protection (namely Sergt. Carlile's wife and Ens. Johnstone's whore) [and] that the prisoner came up and wished that the Carriole, horse and all, might break in & go under the ice, with other insolent Language.

The Prisoner being put to defence denys the crime & says he will not be tryed by a Regimental Courtmartial, but desires a general one, & objects to Ens. Johnstone, for reasons he now will not mention. The Court is of oppinion the prisoner is guilty of the crime laid to his Charge, therefore do sentence him to be reduced and serve as private in the Ranks.

Signed/ Lieut. Christie, president

Approved, George Turnbull, Commandant.

Febry 21st. 1771. Ens. Johnstone by threats & promises prevailed upon Sergt. Carlile, by frequent tamperings & Solicitations, to take his wife back again. I imagine upon Examination of this accommodation it will appear equally abominable as the original iniquitous & intrigueing proceedings.

The 23d febry 1771. Ensigns Johnstone & Strickland haveing requested of the commanding officer that Thomas Carlile, late Sergt. in generall Armstrong's Company, should be restored, he is therefore restored to his former rank (after signing, I fancy, uncommon preliminarys dictated to him by the Destroyer of his peace and tranquility). He is to be obeyed as such. One infamous restoration indeed when the terms are narrowly scrutinized.

N. B.: That upon the 26th febry. 1771. Capt. Turnbull, Commandant, Issued verbal orders to Sergt. [Mc]Murray of the General's Company to Erase the proceedings of the Regimental Court Martial concerning Sergt. Carlile's tryal out of the Regimental Orderly book, & if he could, would get it Erased out of the orderly book of the Lieut. Colonel's Company also. Accordingly Sergt. McGann of the Colonel's Company did erase it, without any previous notice given to the officer who commanded the Company. As that officer was not a little surprized at such uncommon proceedings, he immediately confined him in the guard-house, who in his own defence told his officer he received positive orders from the acting Sergt. Major so to do, who had told him it was the orders of the day by the commanding officer, Capt. Turnbull. Upon which the officer commanding the Coll's Company sent for the acting Sergt. Major who acknowledged to him he had received orders from the Commanding officer of the Fort to have the tryall of Sergt. Carlile torn out of the Book of both Companies doing duty in Garrison. Upon which Declaration the officer set Sergt. McGann at liberty.

Michilamackinac, 22d. febry 1771

Sir—

I hope You will pardon my takeing this Liberty to trouble You, but to ease my own mind I cannot avoid it, by the instigation of my own Notions. I was so imprudent to object to Ens. Johnstone's being a member of my Court Martial, altho' I am now well convinced that his own Honnour would not allow him to do anything prejudicial to Justice. The only Excuse I can make to him & Ens. Strickland is that a Woman who I have the greatest regard for distracted me by her imprudent behaviour. This, Sir, I hope in some part will Extenuate my Crimes, & I shall only further beg leave to Ob-

serve that Ens. Johnstone has behaved to me as a good officer, & I have no ground of Complaint against him, & I am extreamely sorry for, & beg his forgiveness & Ens. Strickland's for my past behaveour, which I never will be guilty of again.

I have the Honnour to be, Sir,

Your most Dutifull & humble Servant,

Signed—Tho's Carlile, late Sergt.

To Capt. Turnbull
Commanding at Michilamackinac

The above is a coppy of a Letter directed to Capt. Turnbull by order of Ens. Johnstone.

a true Copy

Signed/ Tho's McMurray
acting Sergt. Major

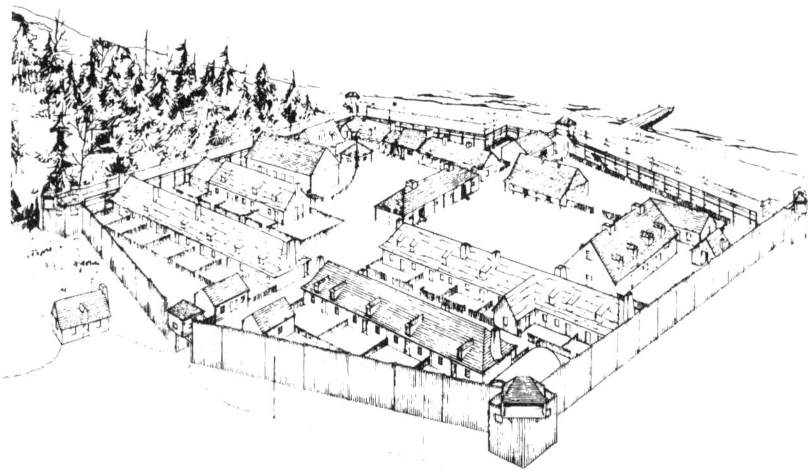

Ft. Michilimackinac during the 1770's

IV

A Catalogue of Foul Deeds

Dr. Morison now summarizes the evidence he had collected against Ensign Johnson into a catalogue of his "exploits." In addition to proving that the ensign was a respecter of no one, regardless of age, rank, sex, or position, the catalogue includes the intriguing report of alleged intimacies between Johnson and Mrs. Robert Rogers. This information may be true since we learn from another source that Major Rogers was said to have been jealous of Johnson. The ironical aspect of this whole matter is that ten years later when Elizabeth Rogers sued for a divorce from the major one of her grounds for the action was that her husband had been unfaithful to her while they were at Michilimackinac.

Ensign Johnson finally met his match in the tough Connecticut trader, Phineas Pond, and resigned his commission in November, 1771, and disappeared from the scene.

Sentencing a soldier to receive a thousand lashes, which Morison also relates in this chapter, was an unusually brutal penalty, although at least one sentence of fifteen-hundred lashes of the "cat" is on record. Ordinarily ten lashes was regarded as sufficient punishment for most offenses and as many as thirty-nine lashes was considered cruel.

". . . sentenced to Receive 1000 lashes for Desertion."

Michilamackinack, 10th Aprile 1771. Ens. Johnstone attempted a rape on a girl betwixt nine & ten Years of age. Her shrieking out Violently alarmed her step-father, Arthur Ross, & others in the barracks. This Arthur Ross was servant to Ens. Johnstone at the time, who upon makeing remonstrances the next morning to Ens. Johnstone of his rude & uncommon behaveour, Received a very severe blow on the left breast from his master, Ens. Johnstone, which made him quit his service instantly.

Ens. Johnstone acknowledged publickly, by way of Bravado, he had carnal dealings with Mrs. Oldham (the mother of this girl upon whom he attempted this Rape) three years agoe, and about twenty Days agoe he vaunted of the same foul deed, declaring publickly it was [no one's business?]. This declaration happened two or three days before he attempted the Rape upon her Young Daughter.

Tuesday the 23d Aprile 1771. We had a kind of horse race here; the most of the garrison walked out to enjoy the pleasure of the Show. Ens. Johnstone being appointed as one of the Judges upon the Occasion, Ens. Strickland's mare was saddled for him, that he might be enabled to execute the important office with the more Alacrity. The racers appeared on the ground expecting Ens. Johnstone with outmost impatience. [They] sent several messages in quest of him; his mare was found; but he himself could not, & no wonder for he was then in a Captain's Cabin marking barrells of Liquor to be Rolled over to the Suttler's house, which was observed to be conveyed in this manner by Creditable Witnesses. Ens. Johnstone seized this opportunity very seasonably while the racers waited half one hour for his Judicial appearance before they could start.

After secureing his Cargoe in this manner he appeared soon after the racers started. The horse won & the mare lost the race (which is a surprizing Circumstance) according [to] the prevailing constitution of this fort.

Thursday 25th. Aprile 1771. A Barrell of Liquor, at least presumed to be, was Rolled over to the Suttler's about 12 o'clock forenoon. This Barrell was marked Capt G. T. [George Turnbull] & rolled over by Donaldson [?] of the General's Company.

A Catalogue of Ens. Robert Johnstone of the 2d. Battl. Exploits.

1. Knocked down a frenchman at Grosse pointe.
2. Quarrelled with Mr. [Alexander] Baxter.
3. Quarrelled with Major [Robert] Rogers, & used uncommon freedom with his wife, common fame says to the extent of carnal conversation with her.

4th. Wounded Corpl. Johnstone of the general's Company in the arm.

5thly. Attempted to draw his sword upon Mr. [Benjamin] Frobisher for which he was put under arrest.

6thly. Quarrelled with & insulted Capt. [Frederick] Spiecmacher [commandant, 1767-68], for which he was under arrest for five months.

7thly. Selling of Common Rum to the Soldiers, mixing water with it, & selling it afterwards at 18. sh. York Currency pr. Gallon.

8thly. Knockeing down Mr. Farrol, Barrack master, betwixt 70 & 80 Years of age, on board of the Gladwin.

9thly. Nonsuited at a prosecution in favours of a prostitute.

10thly. Committed Felony, attempted by him & two accomplices, against the person of Doctor Morison.

11thly. Intended murder by Poison.

12thly. Mixing four ounces of Jallap with the water boiled for Punch at a publick Enter[tain]ment.

13thly. Challenged Lieut. Christie, & asked him pardon without coming to a tryal.

14thly. Sporting with Capt. [John] Browne & Capt. Glazier's Characters, calling the last a mean, low lived, Dirty fellow.

15thly. Flogged Knight, Soldier of the General's Company, by his own hand with a wooden Switch, in presence of Capt. Turnbull without the benefit of a Court martial.

16thly. Kicked & Cuffed Sergeants & Soldiers upon the publick Parade, to which the Commanding officer was present at some of those Irregularitys.

17thly. Attempted to Murder William Morison, Nephew to Doctor Morison, to which Capt. Turnbull, Commanding Officer, was present, with many others.

18thly. Kicked and Cuffed Sergt. Carlile in his own house upon a Sabbath day when the garrison was at Church, & in the Scuffle hurt one of his stones.

19thly. Some days after that he decoyed away the Sergt's wife, Mrs. Carlile, who lived with him upwards of six weeks at Bed & board &c.

20thly. Vaunted he had Carnal dealings with Mrs. Oldham & three Years after attempted a Rape upon her daughter betwixt 9 & 10 years of age.

21st. Was put under arrest by Capt. Turnbull for the space of 24 hours for Quarrelling with Maxwell the Commissary.

22d. Attempted to sow Discord betwixt George McBeath and his wife to whom he offered one hundred pounds &c provideing she would take up with him & quit her husband.

23d. Sergt. Carlile of the General's Company Objected to Ens. Johnstone as a member of a Regimental Court Martial, set upon his Accusation [to] which [he] pleaded not guilty, & for certain Reasons desired the benefit of a general Court martial, which was denyed him.

30th May 1771. That evening after Roll Call, a Delinquent, James Coleman, soldier of the Lieut Colonel's Company, sentenced to Receive 1000 Lashes for Desertion, received near five hundred & would have received more had not I intervened to hinder any more proceedings as he was not able to endure any more.

That very evening of the 30th he was ordered by the Commanding officer to the flogging post to receive the rest of his punishment, without Consulting me whether he was fit to receive them or not. He appeared under a file of men, in presence of the whole garrison, to undergoe that which he was not able to support. At that Juncture, he immediately fell upon his Knees & begged Capt. Turnbull to delay the rest of his punishment till he was more fit to undergoe them. Upon this application Capt. Turnbull asked my oppinion. I answered he was not fit, & consequently he was under the necessity of being carryed home to the Guard house by two soldiers of the guard.

This lenity of mine in favours of the prisoner produced the following Garrison orders (tho' there was no previous complaint lodged):

> *Michilimackinac 31. May 1771. For the future the officer of the Day will visit the men's barracks every forenoon at 12 o'clock to see that the Barracks are kept clean & that the sick or lame are regularly visited by the Surgeon; when prisoners are in that situation the Sergt. of the Guard will report to the officer of the day if it should happen that they are not Regularly attended.*

The 10th of June 1771. Ens. Johnstone quarrelled with Phinehas Pond, a trader from New England. The dispute became very warm with high & insulting Expressions. At length in the height of their dispute Ens. Johnstone took down a brace of pistoles off the chimney brace, presented them to Pond at the Table, challengeing him to take up one of them, which Phineas Pond did directly. Ens. Johnstone in wrath desired Mr. Pond to give his Pistol to Mr. Howard, trader, to charge. He replyed he would not give his Pistol to any man to charge; upon which Pond began to charge his Pistol as fast as he could work. Ens. Johnstone (observeing that Mr. Pond was about chargeing so brisk) took hold of his own pistol by the barrell & pushed the butt of it violently & struck him with great fury in the Pit of the stomach, which staggered him surpriseingly. This unexpected proceeding prevented Pond from loading his Pistol, which he was obliged to drop & make of his hands in his own defence, which he plyed about so manfully that Ens. Johnstone fell flat directly upon the floor. Phineas Pond gave him such terrible bruiseings, black eyes &c. that Ens. Johnstone was obliged to keep his Room for several days, & tho' this day is the 6th. since his disaster, he is not Yet recovered, walking about slowly with a pair of black Eyes. What the consequences of this uggly affair will turn out to I cannot determine.

Ensign Johnstone sold Mr. [Ezekial] Solomon the Jew ninety gallons of common Rum June 1771. The year before he sold fifty bundles of dryed Venison to the said Solomon at 2 sh. & 6d for the benefit of Capt. Turnbull, commanding officer of this Fort.

". . . without these expenses I must starve of cold."

V

Monstrum Horrendum Ingens!

With this partial quotation of a line from Virgil's Aeneid *which refers to the hideous one-eyed monster, Polyphemus, stumbling about after he had been blinded by Ulysses, Morison expresses his opinion of Captain Turnbull. Angered at the treatment he received from Turnbull, the surgeon's mate presumably pictured his commanding officer as a monster, blind to the needs of his men.*

George Turnbull had received his commission in the Royal Americans in 1756 at the time this famous fighting force was being recruited "to avenge Braddock's defeat." In 1758 he had been wounded in the costly British attack on Ticonderoga. After the French and Indian War, Turnbull was promoted to captain in 1765, and before coming to Michilimackinac in 1770 he had been the commander at Detroit for three years. While at Detroit he had been involved with some of the local citizens in a dispute over property rights on Belle Isle, but, according to the adventurer, Jonathan Carver, who visited Detroit in 1768, Turnbull was respected by the inhabitants and traders "for the propriety of his conduct." This record should be borne in mind as one reads what Morison has to say about Turnbull.

Michilamackinac July 9th. 1771. Betwixt the hours of 3 & 4 [in the] afternoon, Capt. Turnbull sent for me to his house upon an affair in which he had not the least concern. No sooner I appeared than he Opened upon me with Volleys of scurrilous Language (in presence of Lieut. Donald Mc-Alpin of the 2d. Battn.) viz: That I was a scandalous fellow, a man of no principles, of a bad heart &c. lastly ordered me go out of his house & commanded me to keep my Distance, which I am determined punctually to observe.

N. B.: All these Epithets (to the conviction of many) are imputations that more peculiarly belong *altenarly* [alternately?] to himself when his character is canvassed by proper judges. If [such things as] Oppression, Detraction, Melediction, Violence, fornication, adultery, breach of Sabbath, tradeing, selling of common rum, Molasses, Wine, Spirits &c, Supporting a Suttlery in which he himself is principally [interested], which is Diametrically opposed to a Military Character, [be considered], he himself is justly entitled to these Epithets & imputations which cannot be attended with much difficulty to prove. Upon these considerations I left his house, whose dirt I shook off from my feet & left the Dirt where I found it. Monstrum horrendum Ingens!

The 26th. augst. 1771. Sent the weekly return by my servt. as I happened to be sick on that morning. Capt. Turnbull enquired of my servt. what my sickness was. My servt. answered, it was a severe attack of the Rheumatism to which I was subject. The Commandant asked my servt. if he could cure me. My servt. replyed he would if he could. After many frivolous questions of this nature, he at last ask[ed] him what did he think I deserved, to which my servt. Replyed, he did not know, "but Sure I am Sir, my master deserves well at my hands."

Upon Tuesday the 17th. Sept. 1771. Capt. Turnbull after Roll Call sent the Sergeant Major to acquaint me he wanted to speak to me. Accordingly I appeared. Then Capt. Turnbull in presence of Lieut. Christie, Ens. Graham and Ens. Strickland asked how I came to move to another house without his leave, & I answered that I thought there was no necessity of giveing any trouble to him for removeing to good Quarters, which I hired for the Winter as there was no possibility of liveing for the Winter in that house Which he ordered me to, May last; especially as both of them were the property of traders in this place & tho' I applyed to him last fall for a Room in the officers' Barracks, as there was one Vacant then, as he did not grant this I thought I had a Right to provide myself the best I could.

He told me [that] tho' I have been so long in the army I made a[s] great progress in the knowledge of my duty as I did in that of my profession, meaning in which I appeared to be equally ignorant. (So far according to the Sultan.)

"I suppose," says he, "You want I should put You into arrest, that You may be exempted from Your duty. But," continued he, "I will not do You that Honnour. You are not worth my Notice. I hope You will not give me the trouble to provide a Room to provide for You next summer."

I told him I'd give him as little trouble as possible and that I'd endeavour [to do] the best I could for myself, tho' at the same time I beged leave to observe that I thought (while I continued to act in the King's Service) I had a right to a room in the King's barracks, which benefit was never granted me during his incumbency. He Replyed he did not chuse to hear any more upon the Subject, and ordered me to be gone, which I did quietly, in presence of the abovesaid gentlemen.

N. B.: When upon application last fall to Capt. Turnbull for a Room in the King's Barracks, which he did not grant, I then applyed to him if he would please speak to influence Mr. Cardin to give me his house for last winter. He gave himself not the least trouble about the matter, in consequence of which I was necessitated to provide for myself. [I] obtained the house from Mr. Cardin, where I lodged Comfortably last winter. As I was obliged to pass the winters preceeding most wretchedly in old houses, not habitable, notwithstanding of my Disbursements on many repeated reparations, such as thatching with Bark, Claying &c, as without these expenses I must starve of cold & every shower of rain [came] in upon me, as also snow drift[ed in] from every quarter when the wind blew high.

Upon Sunday the 1st December 1771. The officer of the day was ordered to place Centrys at different corners of the Garrison upon four or five houses, upon suspicion they smuggled some common rum to entertain them[selves] at such a particular Season, as one of the Sub-Suttlers did not Chuse to sell or had orders [not] to sell under a Dollar each quart.

A soldier and his wife with his Children [were] ordered to their barracks, tho' there was not a drop [of] liquor found in his house. The officer of the day upon entring the room of Fiddler, one of the Royal Artillery, who was enjoying himself with one of his Comrades in garrison [with some rum] which he had purchassed from the Sub-Suttler. [The bottle of rum] was broke to pieces [by the officer] which put a stop to the entertainment tho' they were all quite sober.

All this is supposed to proceed from the orders of the grand Suttler [Captain Turnbull], who did not Chuse that any individual should interfere in diminishing the grist which has been a long time now comeing into his Mill & which he wants to keep agoing for his own particular private interest.

December 15th. Mr. Harise, the interpreter, was committed to the common guard-house by Capt. Turnbull where he remained from eight o'Clock in the afternoon till ten next morning, for beating of a trader's *Engagee* [an *engagé*, one of the French boatmen who were hired to paddle the traders' canoes], tho' many Circumstances of the most Extravagant enormitys have been overlooked in this odious garrison during Capt. Turnbull's Incumbency.

Ensign Strickland [was] put under arrest by Capt. Turnbull's order for useing Sergt. Lewis ill upon his Guard, & the said Ensign continued under his arrest untill he made proper Condescensions to the Sergt. & Yet Ensign Johnstone would not be put under arrest by Captain Turnbull (tho' properly applyed to) for shedding the blood of a gentleman more usefull to the King's service in garrison, more than both, which can be proven to a Demonstration, time & place Convenient.

N. B.: July 2d. 1772. I have now [served] going on four years here, & during that period of time have neither received wood, nor chairs, table, tongs, Dogirons, pockers, &c. from the Barrack master nor any lodgeing in the King's Barracks or from the King, notwithstanding my frequent applications, but was obliged to Lodge in old french Houses, not habitable, at a Vast Expense out of my Pay, by Plastering, thatching &c. to preserve myself from the Inclemency of the Winter Season, which is generally very intense here, and which continues upon average about the space of eight months.

Notwithstanding so badly was I used, on account of provideing of aforesaid lodgeings, haveing not beforehand informed Capt. Turnbull of my intention of providing said Lodgeing for hire, he sent a Sergeant for me to [attend] the Publick parade, where to my surprise in presence of the officers of the Garrison & others he gave me very abusive & Scandalous Language, unbecomeing the Expressions of a gentleman, & when offering to speak in my own Defence, I was ordered Silence! & that he desired for the future I should give him no more trouble about Lodgeings. [He] ordered me about my business, that he would not put me under arrested as he knew that was what I wanted, but would not do me that Honnour. I was not worth his notice.

N. B.: Ensign Strickland & Ens. Graham were put under arrest for differences subsisting among them at his house, which Capt. Turnbull approved of till their differences were settled.

Conclusion

Daniel Morison's journal ends at this point. After July 2, 1772, we lose sight of the unhappy surgeon's mate. It appears at least that he did not remain much longer at the Straits for later that year the various units of the Second Battalion of the Royal Americans were assembled from Niagara, Fort Michilimackinac, and other frontier posts and shipped off to serve in the balmier climate of the West Indies.

Captain Turnbull retired from the army in 1775 by selling his commission, but some of the others who had served at Michilimackinac remained with the Royal Americans and fought in the Revolutionary War. Turnbull's predecessor as commandant, Beamsley Glazier, distinguished himself in the fighting around Savannah, Georgia, in 1779, by leading three companies of the Royal Americans in a fierce charge which drove the American and French forces into headlong retreat and caused the Allies to lift their siege of the British troops in the city. Ensign Johnson's erstwhile comrade-in-arms, John Christie, fought gallantly in 1780 at Mobile in a futile effort to beat off a Spanish attack on that port. Christie thereby redeemed his reputation which had been badly tarnished by his premature surrender to the Indians when he was in command of a fort at present-day Erie, Pennsylvania, in 1763.

Many changes took place at Michilimackinac after 1772, so many, in fact, that John Askin, an old-time resident, in 1778 wrote to Thomas McMurray, apparently the former acting sergeant-major who had retired to a business in Montreal, that he would scarcely recognize the post any more. In place of the drafty old houses, such as the ones Morison had lived in, the people, Askin reported, were "now building tolerable good ones."

The fort also had a new surgeon's mate—another Scotsman, David Mitchell. Unlike his compatriot Morison, Mitchell adjusted very well to the rough conditions of life on the fur-trading frontier. He married a Chippewa woman, and when his regiment was transferred elsewhere he received special permission to stay on as surgeon's mate so that his wife would not be separated from her people. He remained in the area in various capacities until his death in 1830. By then old Fort Michilimackinac had been abandoned for a half century and only a few ruins sticking out of the sand reminded the occasional visitor of the colorful days of the 1760's and 1770's.

Appendix

Historians recently discovered in the Frederick Haldimand Papers of the British Museum in London a document which sheds additional light on the obscure life of Daniel Morison. The document is a petition written by Morison to Frederick Haldimand in Quebec. The document is undated.

To His Excellency Frederick Haldimand Captain General and Governor in Chief in and over His Majestys Province of Quebec, and the Territories depending thereon, in America, Vice Admiral of the same, General and Commander in Chief of His Majestys Forces, in the said Province and the Frontiers thereof etc, etc, etc.

The Memorial of Daniel Morrison Humbly Sheweth That your Excellency's Memorialist was appointed surgeon to six independent Companies raised in Scotland in the Year 1746, and reduced in two Years thereafter, That in the year following he was appointed surgeon's Mate to Lord Loudon's Highland Regiment soon afterwards reduced; That in the year 1757 he came to America as Mate to Lieut. Colonel Frasor's Regt. That during the Winter 1760, he Passed an examination as surgeon, and received that appointment to the 35th Regiment from His Excellency General Murray, which the then Commander in Chief did not confirm, That at the reduction of the 78th Regiment of Foot he was appointed surgeon's mate to the 2d Battallion of the 60th Regiment in which he had the Honor to serve untill the Regiment was ordered for the West Indies where he Could not attend them, on account of His health And that during the Blockade of this City in 1775 he carried Arms, which extraordinary last Fatigue reduced his health and strength still lower. He now most humbly Pray Your Excellency's attention to the length and nature of his Services, and to his advanced time of life, and that you will be pleased to honour him with some marke of your Favour, and your Memorialist as in duty bound Shall ever pray — DAN MORISON SURGEON

British Museum, Haldimand Papers, ADD Manuscript 21,877, p. 440

Index

About the hour o eleven O'clock, Ens.n Robert Johnstone (who for ought I know misled himself Seamen) accompanied by Ens.n John Strickland, & Mr. Mann, we continued there, till about one O'clock in the Morning, when numbers of our Company thought proper to Retire; I proposed retiring also, but Isaac Todd insisted upon my spending one hour or two more with them, rather than Disoblige I consented; about half an hour after Ens.n Johnstone, asked the Company how they liked [illegible] them, they Answered well enough, then he the [illegible] Ens.n Johnstone, blabbed out publickly, Va[illegible]ly & wantonly, he had mingled four Ounces of [illegible] with the water, that was a boiling for proportioning the Punch & Sangary, this giddy Declaration, instead of meeting with Approbation, occasioned the interjection of an Universal Sneer. I said nothing tho' I perfectly knew, such irregular proceedings could not be intended for good, therefore I silently wink'd over it as Others did, at the same time took particular Notice, that Ens.n Johnstone, drank Nothing but Wine all the Night over. ——

John Chinn and Hiatt Oaks who left the Company about one O'clock, seemingly fuddled, returned to the charge one hour & one half thereafter, the aforesaid, John Chinn appeared to be as correctly as ever, in short conversation became very insipid Drinking was the principal Amusement, Varnished over with various inconsistencys, at length time Dragged on very heavily; Consequently I excused